Baby Don't Fall Again

Just Bae

Copyright © 2022 by Just Bae

All rights reserved.

No part of this book may be reproduced in any form or by any electronic or mechanical means, including information storage and retrieval systems, without written permission from the author, except for the use of brief quotations in a book review.

Contents

Prologue	1
Chapter 1	5
Chapter 2	10
Chapter 3	18
Chapter 4	25
Chapter 5	34
Chapter 6	40
Chapter 7	48
Chapter 8	55
Chapter 9	62
Chapter 10	70

Prologue

Life is full of choices, most are simple, like "Do I turn left or right?"

Others are more complex. Then there are the ones you don't want to take, that sometimes end in a very successful conclusion.

Today was definitely one of those successful conclusions. Despite having taken a very dubious choice to join this particular ski trip.

Skiing towards me down the piste was the petite, five foot high, ski Barbie girl, clad in all in black, tight ski gear, with her blond braided hair flapping behind her. She came right up to me, stopping abruptly to hug and reach up to kiss me fully on the lips, laughing. Having been on many ski trips, this was not a common occurrence for me, but one I was happy to endure.

"Thank you. Me Katrina, much happier now. I feel

better, very safe." She said in an European accent, whilst pecking a kiss on my cheek with her bright red lips.

"Me, er, I'm Dave, this is Tim and Sean," I replied, introducing my two fellow skiers.

I'm a volunteer ski buddy with two disabled standing skiers, and we were high in the Alps, bathed in sunshine, with blue skies overhead, standing in a saddle on the mountain ridge that separates Italy from Switzerland. In front of us beckoned our destination back in Italy and behind us was Switzerland, which we had visited that morning.

Hoping Katrina would make a good choice, I asked, "We are returning to Italy, Cervinia. Do you want to ski back to Italy with us?"

She shook her head, "No, I am tired, no like, but I go to Italy, my chalet in Cervinia."

Opposite us stood a refuge and the top station of the Italian side Gondola, which will take Katrina back down into Italy and the ski resort of Cervinia.

"Katrina, see the refuge, walk there, have a break and coffee, okay? Then catch the gondola there, to take you down to the Plan Maison station. But then only ski blue piste, okay? Only ski the blue pistes." Hoping she will in future stick to pistes more suitable to her level of experience.

"But bend the knees, like this? Not like this." I demonstrated the difference between bending her knees and 'sitting on the toilet'. She laughed at my instruction and gave me another hug and kiss. She took off her skis and started walking over the piste to the timber refuge perched on the far edge of the piste.

Watching her walk away from us, I pondered on all the choices I had taken to reach this point. As Katrina turned to wave goodbye, I hoped we would both meet back up again in the coming week.

Chapter One

Several years ago, I chose to volunteer at a disabled ski club. Now at twenty-three years old, I'm a volunteer adaptive ski instructor, rather than following a professional ski instructor career.

Within skiing circles, this makes me the lowest of the low, because I've not done 'n' number of winter seasons at 'X' resort, nor do I have the international qualifications to run and train an Olympic racing team. The reason for this choice is that I already have a career job. I work at an engineering company that is paying me a wage whilst training me and sending me to school.

Just three weeks ago, I decided to join this ski trip as a favor to one of the several charities I volunteer with. Because it would grant two standing disabled skiers their only opportunity to ski this season. They run this trip only for able-bodied ski friends, and the group comprised several people I don't even like.

So maybe I made the wrong choice, choosing to go. But it would keep me in good favor with the charity, so I hoped it may benefit me in the long run.

Luckily I have a deal with my employer, if I deliver parts to an Austrian customer I could use their van, so long as I didn't trash it. Having already done this before, I had adequate snow chains and van heater, so I can keep in the van to save on hotels when driving down. I left straight after work on Thursday night with my skis and other equipment in the van. Going via the channel tunnel, I arrived at the Austrian customer's factory early Friday afternoon. I then drove on through to Italy.

Being my third visit to the ski resort of Breuil-Cervinia, I was driving a familiar route up the valley. This is the highest Italian resort in the Alps, making it very snowy. The additional benefit is the ability to ski out of Italy, into Switzerland, to possibly the most expensive ski resort of Zermatt. Possibly the most dangerous mountain in Europe, the impressive Matterhorn separates both resorts.

Cervinia is a lovely flowing resort, being more of a large bowl rather than just a narrow single valley. It has some great intermediate pistes, and perfect for the two skiers I will be looking after. They promised me at least two free days to free ski, which I love as I will talk to anyone on a chair lift and always end up meeting and skiing with other single skiers.

One skier's family was funding my hotel bill, so long as I shared a room with him. This choice was simple as it saves me money and Tim is fine with that. Whilst older than me in his late twenties, over 6 feet tall, he is slightly autistic with learning difficulties. But I have shared a space with him previously, and he's no problem. You just have to tell him to shower each day and make sure the others don't take advantage of him; his father is super rich and Tim often buys everyone drinks.

Sean, the second skier in my care, is older than my dad. He is retired and partially sighted. He will struggle in cloudy or low light conditions when requires a target to follow, so I have my bright red ski jacket with me. Sean's a nice guy and knows when he has reached his limit. He prefers to play it safe and ski when the area is not crowded.

* * *

I arrived mid-morning to find the hotel was close to one of the main chair lifts, making the first lift of the day an easy walk in ski boots. So next was to stay in town for rest, beer and a pizza or get half a day skiing in. In the back of the van, I slipped on my ski gear, then went ahead and bought a half-day ski pass from the reception. I then caught the chairlift up the mountain.

The day was sunny with blue skies, giving me perfect snow conditions and with it being change-over day the pistes were empty. I sped around my favorite runs to recover my legs. After a few runs, I went back to grabbing my gear out of the van, then onto the hotel reception to collect my room and locker keys. I put my skis and boots in the locker and went up to the room to meet Tim. The first night was the usual piss-taking from the usual older useless party hangers-on.

However, I found a Londoner across the hall from me who I knew quite well named Boris. He is a 'bucketer' like me as we often work together, both whizzing disabled skiers around UK indoor ski slopes, and European Mountains during ski season. Our disabled skiers sit inside ski chairs (known as 'buckets' or 'sit skis') to enjoy the freedom of skiing that one gets regularly.

Boris has a gift of chatting women up, so I often end up as his 'wingman' when we are out. This meeting reassured me that maybe we had both made the right choice in coming.

***

The first few days were great with us enjoying the conditions. Sean would only ski until lunchtime then return to the hotel. Leaving Tim and I to ski on in the afternoon.

Meanwhile, Boris skied with others. He admitted that they were wearing him out with their constant bragging, despite him being the far younger, stronger and better skier. He was looking forward to taking over from me to ski with Tim & Sean later in the week.

* * *

On Monday, Boris and his skiers had gone into Switzerland, returning with glowing reports of excellent conditions and empty pistes.

That evening, Tim asked if we could go to Switzerland like the others. The weather threatened to worsen later in the week, so it would be better to choose to go sooner rather than later. The run into Switzerland from the Matterhorn ridge would be too hard for Graham, especially with the Zermatt valley beyond being in shade all day, making visibility difficult for him.

Chapter Two

We arrived to Switzerland, climbing up the opposite sunny side of the valley by gondola and a train to reach the Gornergrat Observatory & Hotel. Zermatt has several picturesque mountain cog and wheel railways, and a ride on one would be a bonus for us all. We could ski back down in the sun on easy blue pistes and return by retracing our gondola route to return to Italy. This would avoid Sean skiing in the afternoon shadows in the Swiss valley.

I discussed our preference quietly with Graham, who loved the idea, having never been to the Zermatt side before. Tim was beside himself with excitement and told everyone, bringing him some unwarranted teasing from other 'friends' in the group.

*　*　*

I got Tim up early and we caught the chairlift up to meet the higher gondola, bringing us onto the ridge between the two countries. A short ski down and we caught our first gondola down into Zermatt. All our links worked superbly, with us needing a ten-minute wait for the mountain train up to Gornergrat. Once at the station you get the archetypical view back at the bent pyramid shape of the Matterhorn that was now catching the morning sunshine.

After taking loads of photographs in the perfect sunshine, we brought hot chocolate at the outside bar. We didn't stay too long, allowing us to ski down to get as low as we could whilst still in sunshine. We made our target Swiss Gondola Station as it was being swallowed up by the Matterhorn's shadow, much to Sean's relief.

We then rode the gondola down into the valley. A short walk across the station allowed us to catch the next one up to the glacier. This last leg to the glacier will be the longest, and the views all around are stunning. The Matterhorn Glacier Paradise is the highest point of both resorts at 3883m (12740 ft). From there, we drop 400m in height down a steep red link piste through a saddle on the mountain ridge to return into Italy.

Exiting, we walked through a tunnel in the mountain peak for about two hundred meters to the restaurant there. It was busy, and they were refusing entry to anyone who hadn't a reservation. As I stepped out onto the piste, I discovered why.

Despite low winds and great conditions lower down, there was a force ten gale carrying shards of ice, sandblasting you. We would have to brave this for about five hundred meters of link piste until the piste dropped below a mountain ridge to shelter skiers. Choosing this route today was a bad idea.

I explained to Tim and Graham what they would have to do and it would be daring to say the least. Once down, we would be back in Italy with other restaurants available to us. I knew they were capable and trained to ski the distance.

I advised Tim knew he would have to use a wide 'V' shaped snowplough down the narrow link piste, which would to be icy. With our snoods or scarves pulled up to cover our chins and noses, and goggles pulled down, we stepped out into the bracing icy wind.

* * *

It was a battle to get our skis on whilst fighting the wind on hard-packed ice, not being able to get ski poles stuck in, so I had to help Sean and Tim. We edged forward trying to make progress, leaning against the wind. I skated along on my ski's keeping ahead of them, acting as a target for Sean to follow.

The narrow link had a drop of thousands of meters down on the right-hand side. I hopped between the icy piste and fluffy edge to keep my speed down. There was only one skier ahead of us, a small black-clad skier, who judging from their skiing, was beyond their capabilities.

Luckily, I chose to snowplough in the fluffy snow behind her. Enjoying ogling her pert bottom in her tight black pants, Tim and Graham caught me looking. The woman was very petite with a long blond French braid hanging from the back of her helmet. She could have been a real version of a Skier-Barbie.

I cynically thought 'more money than sense,' as she struggled amidst the bad conditions. We were now dropping out of the wind with a flat area of piste five hundred meters down from us.

Leaning backwards, the woman panicked on the steep link. This is a typical beginner's mistake, 'sitting on the toilet' rather than bending her knees. This resulted in her losing her control and balance. She fell back to sit sharply down onto the piste, with her skis pointing downhill. Her shoulders were bobbing up and down, shaking her further downhill and closer to the steep drop off to the one side.

This was an easy choice to make, and I'm always willing to save a damsel in distress. I checked behind to jog out skiing passed and turned uphill into a reversed 'V', snow plough to catch her. As her ski tips reached me, I rotated them ninety degrees to the slope to bring her to a halt. Tim and Sean had stopped behind her, allowing any skiers behind to ski passed to one side.

I asked Tim & Sean to ski down to the flat area further down and wait for me. They gave me a series of helmet nods and passed to drop further down. I looked back at my little ski Barbie, black-clad, trapped, fallen skier. Like us, her snood was covering her face, and she had the latest gold reflective goggles down over her eyes. Her shoulders were still bobbing up, she was sobbing. I made a calming motion with my arms.

"Calme s'il vous plaî," I said hoping she understood French.

"Calmare per favour," I repeated in case she understood Italian.

"Ok, thanks," replied a quiet voice that I could barely hear over the noise of the wind.

The woman pulled her snood down and propped her goggles up. Exposing the prettiest face I have ever seen, better than any button-nosed Disney princess in any picture. But with tears streaming down her red face, she was still blubbering.

"Ok? Calm down, you're safe, I have you. Are you hurt?"

"No, no. I'm okay."

"Where are your friends?" I asked.

The woman pointed down to the flat area, where there

were quite a few groups of skiers, including Tim and Sean. She then said quietly, "My Brozer."

Ok, so maybe Polish (as the Poles like to ski Italy, but then so do many other Eastern European countries).

The woman then blubbered out a few more sobs, still looking frightened.

"It's okay, I'm a ski instructor," I lied. I hoped that my red jacket and ski pants, similar to Swiss instructors, gave her some assurances.

"If you're not hurt, can you stand?" I asked.

The woman nodded *okay*. Looking up, I could now see quite a few groups, braving the conditions, making their way out onto the glacier above.

I held my hands out to hold hers, leaned back to pull her up to stand. The woman popped up as she weighed almost nothing.

"Ok, very good, can you rotate your skis to make a snowplough again?"

The woman nodded *yes*.

I let go of her hands and slid backwards to give her room and motioned with my hands, how I wanted her to rotate her skis. With a nod, she copied my instructions until she was holding a wide 'V' snowplough above me.

I looked into her eyes and asked if she was okay. She looked more confident and nodded.

"Okay, I will stay in front, we will slowly ski down, lean forward," as I leaned forwards to show her.

The woman shook her head, still not confident. So I started a slow slide backwards, keeping one eye on her and one on people descending way above us. Even though the link was still steep, she kept a slow controlled speed. Anytime I saw the woman lean backwards, I would shout a warning to encourage her to correct it. Not wanting a repeat of her falling.

As the link levelled and widened to join the flat area, I stepped aside to ski alongside, encouraging her. Once on the flat wide area, with her heading towards a single waiting skier, I skied on to join Graham and Tim again.

When we were about to set off once more, I looked around to check that Skier Barbie was safe. But her brother had already left and was skiing off, out of control of himself. The woman stood there terrified once more, watching him disappeared around the corner. Giving me another set of choices to make.

Sean was getting cold, so I explained the next far easier and wider stage of the route to him. Luckily there was a yellow jacketed skier near a piste signpost that I used as a marker for him. They both set off to the next junction to bear left into Italy.

I chose to once again to ski over to my damsel in distress and joined her, as she looked pleading at me with her eyes.

"It's okay. I can ski with you. Can you ski parallel?" I

asked, placing my skis parallel to each other, hoping the young lady understood. Although she still looked unsure.

"You know Parallel, like chips?" I showed the shape made by skis, parallel to each other. We often use the terms Pizza & Chips when teaching to show the shape we need the skis to be in.

The woman laughed, "Oh yeah, like Chipz."

So I set off, exaggerated my turns to emphasize how she should mimic me. The woman laughed and then followed. She could parallel ski but was still uneasy. She was very much a novice and should not have been at this height or skiing this class of piste. By the third turn, the young lady was copying me and growing more confident. I ensured she put in lots of turns to then finally scoot in a straight line to join Tim and Sean waiting at the signpost.

And that reader is where you joined me, with Ski Barbie Katrina skiing towards me for a hug and a kiss. As you can see, it took me several selections of various choices, good and bad, to reach this point. But from here on in, was I able to meet Katrina again?

Chapter Three

I indicated to Tim to set off and checked Sean was ready, then off we skied back into Italy. Leaving Katrina behind, having forgotten to even try to arrange to meet her later.

We found a good restaurant for a long lunch, then we dropped Sean off back at the hotel around two. Tim elected to stay with Sean at the hotel as he was also beat. I chose to take advantage of the freedom and shot off to hunt out some more testing, steeper pistes.

As the afternoon wore on, I kept high up the resort, to drop lower as the higher lifts close. I skied down to check one chair lift, but it had already closed with. A nearby restaurant was now an après-ski bar, and I could hear some stomping club beats coming from it. So I avoided the choice of going lower down and diverted to the restaurants outside terrace après-ski bar.

I set my skis and poles in an empty place in the snow

and walked through the gateway onto the external terrace bar. A complete range of age groups littered the busy terrace area, the majority dancing and drinking. I made my way to the bar to get a beer and wandered around, enjoying the atmosphere.

A shout rang out above the noise, "Daaaf." But I ignored it. "Daaaf." The shout was louder and bursting out of the crowd came Katrina. Now helmetless, with her braided hair bobbing, looking even more stunning than before. Her arms wrapped around my neck and she gave me a big hug and kissed me on the cheek.

Wow, I was winning today.

"Daaaf, I'm happy you iz ear. Cum, cum," she grabbed my arm and led me through the crowd to a group of five girls flanked by some pissed-looking guys. One was standing back, looking rather sheepish. Judging from the colours of his ski jacket and pants, he appeared to be the brother who left Katrina on the piste.

Katrina led me over to a tall, unattractive, angry-looking guy who was taller than me, "My ozer brozer, Petri."

Petri held his hand out and I shook it, not sure where this was going, then he laughed, "Haha, you Daaaf?"

"No, Dave, my name is Dave."

"Haha, my sister's English is terrible. She said you saved her?" His face now changed, becoming more pleasant.

Taking his queue, so did the rest of the group. The girls burst out in some Eastern European chatter with Katrina, who kept hold of my arm. I felt like an animal being paraded for sale, as the conversation was obviously about me.

"Yes, she had fallen, I couldn't choose to leave her," I said.

Then the conversation turned to me as if I was a celeb.

I told the group that I was from the UK and as soon as I mentioned that, Katrina's brother interrogated me on what I do for a living. I make it a rule never to tell the exact truth in these situations, as you never know your interrogator. I kept it simple stating that I worked in London generally, keeping the lies simple and easy to explain away as a 'misunderstanding' if ever found out.

The more we spoke, the more Katrina's brother seemed alright. The group were from Poland. Petri's friends eventually introduced themselves, but it was a rapid machine-gunfire of names which I could never pronounce or remember.

Suddenly a tray of shots appeared between us, and I was offered one. Petri clarified that I was their guest of honour as I saved his little sister. I was getting a little worried about how 'little' she was. She was getting very touchy and stayed at my side whilst keeping up a steady flow of unpronounceable Polish. The age of the group seemed to be around the mid-20s, with Petri looking the eldest.

But the range of girls looked to be anything from eighteen to early twenties. With Katrina being the smallest, she seemed younger, making me nervous. It didn't seem as if it would take much to upset her brother, and he was way bigger than me.

"You're a ski instructor?" Petri asked. So I had to explain my profession a bit. Explaining that I was a disabled ski instructor in England and the two men I was skiing with are disabled. He immediately translated for the non-English speakers around. The group all nodded, making Katrina hold tighter onto me, just in case any of her friends were in any doubt that I was hers!

Soon another shot was offered and drunk, warming me throughout. Katrina was keeping up with her share, so I was still unsure over her age. The alcohol and music were taking effect and as we all talked, I joining the group dancing to the music. The conversation was straightforward, either through pidgin English to Katrina or English to Petri.

Katrina unwrapped her arms from me and the group of girls left with the trays to buy the next round of drinks. Petri came over asking me about his little sister, "You like my little sister?"

The beer and shots caught up with me and my

bravado, "Yeah, I do, but how 'little' is she? I don't want to be in trouble because you're a lot bigger than me!"

Petri thought I was funny, telling the group in Polish, who joined him in the joke, but not answering my question. Another tray of drinks appeared in front of us, carried by the brace of women.

Katrina wrapping her arms around me and kissing my cheek, "Miss me?" Petri rattled out his version of my question in Polish to all the girls. Who all screamed with laughter looking at Katrina.

"You silly boy, I am nineteen years. I'm a student sports instructor, learning English, possible to work in London?" Katrina said, leaning up to kiss me, first on the cheek then on the lips, tasting of strawberry. I felt relieved, as now I could relax. On queue, I picked up the next shot glass and we all drank, then the next, both containing some strong strawberry liquor.

* * *

Through the crowd, I saw Boris. Feeling in the need for some support, I called him over, to be my wingman for a change. His face shocked at the brace of lovely girls in the group I was with.

As soon as I explained and Petri translated, the girls flocked around him, with the taller one called Celek, seeming to win him. "It looks like you have won second place, Boris," I told him, as Petri introduced everyone to my friend.

Katrina's friend, Celek paired up with Boris. She had jet black short hair, just covering her ears, being taller than Katrina at 5 foot 6. She had a fuller figure than Katrina, more hourglass-shaped with nice C-cup boobs coming out of her ski jacket and a nice pear shape holding together her ski pants.

I caught Boris up to speed and he told me that tomorrow, he could take Tim and Sean. Petri overheard and asked if I could ski with them tomorrow, as Katrina could use some help. Katrina was excited at the prospect, "Yes, tomorrow we ski, you teach me?"

"Yes, yes...I teach you tomorrow," I replied. *Well, how could I refuse that pretty face as she hugged me...*

Boris was also given a shot glass and was included in the pidgin English and Polish conversations. We all jigged and danced to the thumping music under the Italian facade of the Matterhorn. Katrina was being very affectionate, whether dancing or stood talking, he would kiss and cuddle at every opportunity. Either her English or my hearing improved the more we drank.

As the terrace thinned with the light deteriorating, a few of the older 'friends' came over. Showing obvious jealously, because of the bevvy of gorgeous Polish girls we were with. They tried to be our 'best friends' despite their previous duplicitous behaviour on other trips. I explained to Petri and after a burst of Polish, they were all given the cold shoulder, they took the hint and left.

Now the sky was darkening and with the flat light on the snow. Petri said to join them at a pop-up shot bar in the town, then afterwards for dinner in their chalet. His father owned the chalet, and they had enough room.

Boris and I were still in ski gear, and after an hour or more of dancing, I needed to get out of my boots. We agreed to meet up at the pop-up bar and offered directions. As we left to gather our skis, Katrina came over and gave me a passionate French kiss. She was chuckling as her hand innocently palmed my cock. It was bulging nearly out of my ski pants.

Chapter Four

Boris and I skied like demons down the piste to reach our hotel and ran the last hundred yards to the boot room. Leaving our boots and skis in lockers, we then dashed upstairs to our rooms. Not bothering to shower, we changed into more relaxing attire. Boris gave me a handful of his emergency condoms as we threw ourselves down the stairs to see the organiser.

Over jeering and jealous taunts in the hotel bar, we explained that we were both on promises, so they weren't to wait up for us. I spoke to Tim and told him I'll see him in the morning. Sean was sympathetic and said he would make sure Tim was okay.

Boris and I ran a sprint down the hill into the town centre. We found the pop-up bar busy with crowds outside but bouncers on the door not letting anyone in. Inside, we spotted Petri, and I waved catching his attention. He got up and walked to the door, beckoning me and Boris. He said something quickly to the bouncers and they opened the door to let us in.

"It's okay, my father is a friend of the bar owner," Petri told us. He shook our hands and led us through the steaming throngs of people inside, all still in ski gear.

Katrina and her friends were all sitting at a table at the corner of the bar. It was like a boob festival, with nipples protruding everywhere. Katrina still looking every bit the life-size ski Barbie. No longer in her jacket, she had the tightest sports wicking sleeved top on, showing her sports bra and pert B-cup jugs trapped inside.

Boris had to shout in my ear to make himself heard, "Fuck, all our Christmas's at once, you are the best mate ever."

I embraced him and said, "you owe me one, bro."

I then edged around the table to sit next to Katrina, passing her my jacket, to add to the pile behind her. She hugged me and gave me a long kiss, being able to taste that strawberry liquor again.

Boris was getting the same treatment from Celek. Petri returned with a round of drinks. We all joined in the bar's energy, dancing on stools and tables, singing, shouting and laughing, enjoying every minute.

Others in the group were already couples and happy that Boris and I had paired up the last two of their remaining single friends. Sitting next to Katrina, she wasn't slow at being forward. Her hand playing over my throbbing cock beneath the table. Smiling at the results and kissing me whilst whispering Polish and English in my ear.

To distract myself, I started explaining our skiing plans for the season which impressed the group. As I told the group that two weeks earlier we had been skiing in Austria, and in a month, I will be back in France for two weeks, they wooed. Boris and I showed them photos and videos of us both bucketing various disabled skiers all over the resort.

All the time, Katrina was toying with my cock under the table. The bar was rocking to the thumping club music with the group singing to the Euro-Songs and revelling in the party. She even had taken my hand and placed it between her legs. Being short with thin legs, I could work her pussy but could only imagine its wetness beneath her pants. She unzipped me and her small hand worked its way in to grab my cock to play with it.

I looked across the table and Boris was receiving similar treatment, judging from his raised eyebrows when he saw me looking at him.

In a lull in the music, we heard a knocking on the window near us. Through the condensation, we saw some of our hotel 'friends' waving, asking to gain them entry into the bar. We chose to stick two fingers up to them and laughed, ignoring their pleas. Petri thought this was great, laughing and being the closest, slapping Boris on the back.

My stomach was now growling and the reality of having too much drink and not enough food was making itself plain. In time, Petri brought two gigantic pizzas and garlic bread to the table.

Despite his gruff exterior, he was a nice guy, with us both getting on well. His initial gruffness towards me must have been a natural protective defence of his little sister. He told me that he had served several years in the Polish army and now married. He decided to help his father in their family business. His father had been a coal miner but started a pig farm. He now is one of the largest pig farmers in Poland, hence owning the chalet.

* * *

No sooner as we had devoured our food, Petri answered a call and told us we were about to go. Leaving the bar to hit the frosty night air, making you realise how much we had drunken. I didn't feel a thing. Petri then directed the group to a large mini-bus taxi which was waiting to take us to their chalet on the edge of the town. My earlier research into the area suggested that they stayed on the side of the lower piste which was reeking of millionaires.

Boris read my mind telling me, "For God's sake, please don't piss off Katrina. We could be out of our depth here, mate."

"Too late, we're in this now!"

* * *

We all decanted from the mini-bus in pairs. We entered the chalet via their boot room, which was massive compared to the ones I have used before. They gave Boris and me hotel-style guest slippers before we took our trainers off. We helped the girls out of their boots and they pulled us into the main hallway.

"Ah, the hero of the day," boomed the voice from a large-bearded man. He introduced himself as Katrina's father, grabbing my hand to shake it. "My useless son regrets his stupidity and I welcome you and your friend, as our guests tonight.

"Come inside." He introduced us to Katrina's mother. Walking us into a lounge area to introduce us to more people, who had more unpronounceable Polish names. Petri introduced us to his wife, who informed us that the staff wouldn't have dinner ready for a while.

* * *

Katrina came into the lounge, having changed into leggings, and her dark-brownish hair was now loose, running down her back to below her shoulder blades. The room erupted in another round of machine-gun rapid-fire of Polish conversation as Katrina explained her rescue to everyone in the room. Once finished, she hugged me and asked me to show her father the ski photos of Boris and I from Austria. Soon questions bombarded us as the staff brought us more drinks.

As the conversation died, Celek entered, having also changed into leggings. She gathered Boris, spoke with Katrina, and we were both led out back towards the boot room. Passing the boot room, we entered what must be a spa area, with timber-clad rooms. Cubby shelves held clothes, and they offered us ones to use that held clean towels for us.

Katrina and Celek shed their clothes to reveal they both had the tiniest bikinis beneath. They stowed them into the cubbies and took the towels. Boris looked at me and there was no way I was going to miss this. I was already down to my boxers, trunks or not, I was going with the girls. Boris shrugged and commented, "When in Rome..."

The girls giggled at our lack of trunks and led us through a door to walk through a shower and into the main spa area. Both had the most admirable bum cheeks and once wet, were stunning.

Already sat in the largest hot tub I have ever seen, were four pairs of their friends. Girls were all sat on their boyfriend's lap. So Boris and I sat in spaces to have Katrina and Celek lower themselves onto our laps. Petri entered with his wife and several bottles of champagne and glasses to join us. Katrina was enjoying rubbing her bubbly, tight cheeks on my dick. Judging from the bobbing of the other girls, she wasn't the only one teasing her mate.

"First to cum must drink the water, then we can all cum and you still drink!" laughed Petri. "And then you clean the filter." The group all laughed, with all the girls wiggling their rumps to see if anyone was going to lose the bet. We all had flutes of champagne and continued the party. Katrina continued to tease with her cheek clenching.

"You want a massage?" Katrina asked, clenching her cheeks on my cock. As soon as I moaned, "Yes," She stood up and pulled me from the hot tub.

* * *

Grabbing our towels, she walked me into an adjoining tiled room. When she shut the door and locked it, I knew that once again I had made the right choice. She looked impish as she dropped her bikini top onto the floor to release her lovely small pert breasts and display button nipples.

Topless with her loose hair, she was a Barbie goddess. We embraced, and she indicated for me to lie on the massage table. As normal, I led face down. Flying in the face of normality, Katrina pulled my boxers off and enjoyed several strokes of my cock with her soft buttery hands.

She poured a cool mint smelling liquid on my legs and cheeks. Her hands immediately started working my leg muscles. My previous massage experiences told me she was proficient and skilled. Her hands worked up and down my thighs.

Katrina sat up on the table, straddling my thighs. She kneaded my buttocks with her knuckles, then running her hands up the small of my back. I must have moaned in response.

"Mmm, it's good, yes? You're so tight, I loosen your muscles..."

"Mmm, yes, please."

I could feel my muscles knot loosening as the cool oil was now warming deep into my muscles. Her touch though was warming and heating my desire. For such a small girl, she was no weakling. She was a powerful goddess, with her fingers running deep into my flesh and muscles. Her hands reached up to my shoulders and her button nipples dug into me with her soft, small breasts squashed into my back. Katrina repeated this many times, even tracking her nipples over my back like fingernails.

My loins were pumping desire into my shaft and I was aching to go further, hoping to enter her soon. Katrina laughed, enjoying building up my excitement as much as I was. Her fingers continued up my neck and worked their way around my shoulders and neck. The next time she leaned forwards she led flat on my back, her breasts between us. Nibbling my ear, she whispered, "You want to fuck me?"

I had to restrain myself from leaping off the massage table with eagerness.

"Mmm...I can't say no. Can I?"

Chapter Five

I unlocked the door and checked to see who was around. Now the hot tub was empty except for Celek and Boris, who were too busy necking to notice me. I wrapped a towel around me and tiptoed out to check my jean pockets. I found and grabbed a couple of Boris's condoms; I turned and both he and Celek were looking at me, grinning.

"Hey, buddy, I need one of those, too."

So I trotted up and handed him one. Celek touched my hand and asked, "Be gentle with my Katrina. I need her in one piece," She smiled. *Ok, that piled on the pressure.*

As I came back inside the massage room, Katrina pounced on me from behind some cupboards. She wrapped her arms around my neck and hugged me. Her bikini bottom had gone. She smiled as I waved the condom packet at her as an explanation for my absence. Locking the door behind me, I knew exactly what I had to do first. I wanted to practice what two weeks ago I had learned from a German woman in Austria.

I walked Katrina back to the massage table, cupping my hands on both of her lovely cheeks I lifted her onto the table. I lifted her legs onto my shoulders, make her lie on her back. Her lovely small tits exposed to me.

She flicked her hair to create a neat flat star spread of her shining brunette hair around her. Between her legs was a beacon of pink lips, twinkling of nectar that she had already conjured up. Above was a little maker's nameplate of soft, thinned, well-trimmed bonnet hair, with her lovely skin beneath showing through.

I bent down with my head between her legs, sliding my hands around underneath her thighs to above her hips. Caressing her washboard flat stomach, I started licking her inner thighs. To then tracking across her hairline, I could smell perfume.

* * *

The cheeky Polish girl had anticipated all this. I now considered that she may have selected and seduced me, not the other way around. Her body was slowly writhing, and she was moaning anticipating what would happen next. I raised my hands to Katrina's small soft breasts flipping her button hard nipples. They felt like joystick buttons. As soon as my fingers touched them, Katrina twisted and moaned, then I teased them a little.

My tongue was drying. I centred myself and starting at her bonnet ridge I worked down to her pink slightly swollen cunt lips. As my tongue arrived at her purse crease, Katrina gave a sharp intake of breath and groaned. "Oh yes..." she sighed as I worked my tongue slowly, starting at the top, unzipping her on my way down.

Flicking my tongue sideways, Katrina was starting to cream, so that made me want to delve deeper. I found her clit bud already perky, so I teased around it. When I kissed and sucked on it, she squealed, "Wooweee, again." So I did, and again, and again.

Her hips raised, and her hands pushed me downwards. So I licked further down to find her cunt's entrance, extending my tongue as far as I could reach. Katrina was moaning, interjecting her sounds with spoken Polish, which sounded more sweet nothings than obscenities. As she was self-lubricating, it made it easier for me to tongue tease her. Moving from clit to entrance and back, alternating between kissing and sucking, Katrina couldn't remain still.

I then drifted my hand down to play with her. I slipped my finger into her wet, unzipped purse. Flicking and running it around her clit, I followed the path of my tongue. As my finger grazed Katrina's purse, I slowly worked my tongue back up to her nipples. Katrina's hands ruffled and ran through my hair, pulling me down to suck harder.

"Fuck..." I moaned sucking those buttons as my finger slipped into Katrina's entrance below. It was tight, but with her getting wetter by the second, I began pulsing in and out of her rhythmically. Then I was about to put two fingers inside her but she grabbed my hand and pulled it away.

"Mmm David, no!" She quietly pleaded, and then guided my finger to flick between her clit bud and entrance once more.

"Mmm, better, mmm..." Katrina guided my fingers and showed me the technique and pace she desired. The proof was in the pudding. She was moaning more as she arched her back and thrust her hips, grunting Polish words that now sounded like obscenities. Katrina grabbed my head, pulling me up for a kiss.

Thrusting her hips into my finger, I could feel her climax building to such a point I knew she was going to cum. I know I was, and yet my cock remained untouched. As her orgasm built, the sexual tension was electrifying.

Then she pleaded, "Now Dave, put on the condom and let go inside me."

* * *

I couldn't open the packet fast enough. I slipped the condom on and I climbed onto the table on my knees. Leaning over, my hand guided my condom clad cock into her. Katrina's eyes flashed apprehension, then a little grimace of pleasure as I entered and slipped into her tight pussy.

Her face changed to desire, then a big smile grew on her face as her legs wrapped around my back. With unprecedented access into her, I drove in, bottoming out on her cheeks. Whilst the condom insulated me, her pussy walls gripped me, whilst her soft, girlish body writhing beneath me was exquisite.

Her hips were matching my thrusts as we sped up the pace. Her mouth open in ecstasy as she pleaded in between Polish obscenities, "Fuck me, woow, mmph, oh, oh, oh, umph, umph, umph."

Suddenly, Katrina's legs and arms gripped me in a tight bear lock, as her back arched and her muscles wrenched taught, "Yeeeeeessss, yeeeeeessss."

Feeling her grip after that building crescendo, I released my orgasm into the condom. "Fuckkkkkkkk—" I moaned holding the thrust deep into her, whilst kissing her passionately.

"Oh yes, Dave..." she panted as I emptied all of my seed into the condom. "You like, don't you?"

"Hmm...yes...." I managed to say this was the best feeling I had in weeks.

We held the position for a while, then Katrina unwrapped her legs around me and we separated. She was grinning and planting kisses on me whilst we caught our breath. We climbed off the massage table and she pulled her bikini back on, offering me my boxers. We hugged and kissed whilst tidying up the room.

Chapter Six

Outside the spa was empty, but there were groaning and humping noises coming from inside the sauna. Katrina directed me to the toilet, and I binned the condom and freshened up. I joined Katrina back into the hot tub, smiling and talking, the first time we had been alone all day.

We chatted about what she wanted to do in the future. Discussing her training to either become a coach or teaching.

She wanted to come to London to work and asked about where I lived in London and what I do there for a living. I stuck to my original story, using information from Boris. Telling her about the high cost of living and what little I know about the place and the Underground.

I tried putting her off, but Katrina was quite insistent about getting my number and coming to London. I asked her about prospects in Poland and whether she saw a future in helping her brothers and father in the pig farming industry.

Every answer indicated that her mind was set on leaving her country for good.

* * *

The sauna door opened to save me, with Boris and Celek coming out very hot and sweaty. Red faced Boris pulling his boxers up and with Celek still naked laughing at seeing us there. Boris headed to the toilet and Celek walked over with her large tits bouncing. She climbed into the hot tub, not bothering to even try to put her bikini on.

Once again, the two girls rattled off a question and answer routine. Their Polish rattled at machine-gun speed, finishing with the two girls squealing, hugging and kissing. Celek leaned over and sat on my lap embracing me. Not concerned that her exposed breasts and nipples swished across me, giving me a fat kiss on the lips.

"Thanks for being good to my girl, she liked it very much," Celek said.

Katrina shouted at Celek playfully then pulled her off me.

Boris came back shortly after and slipped into the hot tub alongside Celek. I asked Celek what she did for a living, to avoid the conversation returning to questions about London.

Gratefully, she had a lot to talk about, as she works for Katrina's father, helping with the paperwork with the two have been friends since primary school.

A head poked around the spa door to announce dinner would be ready in ten minutes. The girls cheered and ran over to showering room without us. When they were done, Boris and I took our turns, then got dressed casually. The girls were still drying their hair by the time we were ready.

* * *

We arrived in the lounge to find everyone sitting around. Empty seats were awaiting. The meal went on forever and we lost count of the courses, containing lots of things and booze. The atmosphere was quite boisterous, with the ladies holding their own.

Afterwards, we all went into the games room with a large projection cinema screen and had a karaoke dance-off competition. With neither Boris nor I being clubbers, everyone resoundingly beat us. We tried to sing the songs with the lyrics running down the side of the 80-inch screen, and the dance moves were impossible for us to pull off.

The girls even beat the guys in a group sing and

dance-off. Thankfully, being tipsy, we could use it as an excuse. I lost track of all time until I noticed that Boris and Celek had disappeared. Katrina pulled me to the side and suggested we go to her bedroom. When I looked puzzled, she nudged me signalling that it would be okay.

* * *

Anyone who has used an Alpine chalet knows that you can find yourself squeezed in with at least one or three others to a bedroom. I have before now shared with six others in what even in London would be a single bedroom bedsit. Katrina's room was normal single sized, but larger than the hotel room I was sharing with Tim. She even had a sexy-red sofa in its middle.

She undressed in an instant and disappeared under the duvet. I did the same and slipped in to join her. She asked me to repeat my performance from earlier, encouraging my head downwards.

With the lights off and being under the duvet, there were no distractions, except for Katrina's moaning as I licked and pleased her. She liked her nipples to be pulled and my tongue to flit between all her purse's targets. She even briefly rolled over, face down for me to lick her back door.

Whilst not being my first choice of destination for my tongue, I was grateful for her having dabbed some sweet perfume to reward me. She rolled back over and kissed me. Holding my cock that was eager for satisfaction, she asked me to put on another condom.

Once protected, I turned to find Katrina kneeled up, waiting for me to lie on my back. She straddling me with my cock standing to attention, begging to enter her once again. Katrina guided me into her with her soft hands. Her pussy was tight and even through the condom my foreskin was pulled sharply back, she grounded her hips inward. I held onto her slim hips, helping the grind.

Above me, Katrina tried recreating what could be an amateur porno scene. Arching her back, flattening her lovely small breasts, she ran her hands up through her long locks to behind her head, elbows out, exposing her naked armpits. She was a gorgeous Barbie doll, with her long hair hanging draped down her arched back, as she continued to grind our hips together. I reached up to her breasts and squeezed her nipples to excite further, moaning from her small mouth.

"Fuck..." she sighed elegantly.

Suddenly, Katrina's door clicked open, and Celek crept inside, in a bathrobe, giggling.

"Boris went back to the hotel. I heard my friend having sex, so I don't want to be alone. Can I join?" *It appeared that Boris's choice of returning home gave me a bonus.*

* * *

Katrina turned over, reaching her arms out to her friend, inviting her to join us. Celek dropped her bathrobe and she was naked as the day she was born. Celek and Katrina embraced. This was not a friendly drunken kiss on the lips, this was a lover's kiss that they held whilst caressing each other. Celek's hands held Katrina's head, whilst Katrina continued grinding on me. As they made out, Celek's hands slid down Katrina, stealing underneath my hands to rub her breasts, then slide down to her thighs.

Her finger teased between us to flick and tease Katrina's bud, sending shockwaves through her. Her hands then drifted up to my stomach, chest and to hold my head. Lowering herself down on to me, squashing her breasts into me and kiss me on the mouth, her tongue searching mine out. She was so hot with Katrina still riding me.

"Katrina says you have a very nice tongue, I would like it too." Celek moved to climb onto the bed, her nicely round, pear-shaped rump straddling my head. She lowered her pussy down onto my mouth. She was soaking wet and I could taste her cream. I worked my tongue as I had practiced on Katrina. Both Katrina and Celek were moaning loudly now.

I slid my hands up Celek's stomach to hunt out her large soft mounds but found Katrina's hands already caressing them. Katrina was now bouncing on my dick with a little slap as she landed. I felt the two girls lean in to kiss each other and as Katrina landed next; she trapped Celek's hand between us. She was frantically frigging Katrina through an orgasm, giving a muffled scream into Celek's mouth.

"Womph, mmph, mmmmph, mmmm..."

I felt Katrina shudder as the sloppy kisses the two were sharing made loud smacking noises. Katrina, seconds later, got off me. I looked down seeing her pair of slender fingers peeling my condom off.

The same fingers then slid up and down my cock. I felt her soft touch, my excitement now yearning for satisfaction. Katrina and Celek leaned further forward and their lips enveloped my cock, engulfing hard. I directed the back to their heads to what I fancied.

Katrina's arms slid back. I heard her slap Celek's buttcheek making her giggle and moan.

One of their fingers rubbed passed my nose to probe into Celek's backdoor. Celek changed positions and now her wet pussy was grinding on my face. We were officially 69-ing each other whilst Katrina licked and sucked wherever she pleased.

* * *

I kept sucking Celek's cunt knowing I couldn't survive further with their soft, warm lips moving up and down my cock. I was close to releasing but Celek first had hers.

Her orgasm was the creamiest experience I ever encountered; all of her affections were poured out. Katrina spanking her cheeks as she kissed her friend's back. Her finger continually probing inside her friend's back door.

"Mmmmm, mmmph, Kammmph, Kammmps," Celek moaned as her flood continued running down my face. All at the same time, I started coming down both of my company's wet mouths.

"Fuck..." I moaned when Katrina cleaned us both up.

Our bodies were fused for a short while in a confusing granny knot that took a little unravelling once we were finished. We wriggled around for all three of us to link up, spooning under the duvet. Celek was very pleased, sandwiching me between her and Katrina.

Chapter Seven

I woke in the early hours, as the sun was about to peek from behind the mountains. I dressed, leaving Celek and Katrina spooning, and slipped out of the room. It took a few wrong turns to return to the boot room to get my jacket and trainers. It was a sharp awakening as I slipped out of the chalet, into the frosty mountain air. I wound my way back through the streets to our hotel. It was far further than I thought and had to enter my hotel using their boot room security key code and crept up to find Tim still asleep.

* * *

I managed a little sleep until Tim woke me up with his clattering around, so I dressed, and we both went down to breakfast, although I had a bit of a hangover.

Over breakfast, the older skiers moaned at the disappointment of being left outside the bar last night.

Making me happier with my choices. I ignored them and had double helpings of scrambled eggs and bacon, drinking as much tea as I could. Boris came down very late to join us, also receiving some jeering insults. Sitting by me, he asked how much longer I had stayed after doing karaoke. I whispered back about returning to Katrina's room, then a hint of what transpired by saying, "You know Celek swallows?"

"NO, you dog, you didn't?"

"No, she did. After you left, she joined us."

"She was keen for me to leave as soon as we fucked, so she joined you two then?"

It disappointed Boris at having been used. We continued a quickly whispered conversation of both our versions of events.

* * *

Boris and I had several choices for the next day, but we chose to meet for lunch with Tim and Sean. Leaving them, I returned to the hotel to shower and try to catch up on some sleep.

My phone's alarm went off at 9:30, giving me time to get my ski gear and rucksack on, to head to the boot room. I made my way to the pop-up bar for ten. With no one in sight, I ordered a cappuccino and hanged around for a bit.

Not long after Petri, Katrina, Celek and their friends all arrived; unbelievably, none seemed the worse for wear. Katrina in her ski gear, with a new pony tail style bobbing behind her, came over for a hug and a kiss. The guys gave handshakes as they passed and the girls light handshakes and kisses on the cheeks, whilst giving me smiles. We all caught the six-man chair up to the first pistes.

* * *

At the top of the chair, Petri gave instructions and split the group into two. He left me with Katrina, Celek and one of the other girls called Marzena. I felt like Ken with Barbie and her friends as we skied over to a second chair lift to take us higher up. We had a nice flowing run back down to the town on some nice blue pistes to start the day.

The girls weren't that bad at skiing, as they could all parallel ski. They only needed tweaks to their forms and more experience before going higher up. I urged Katrina to use parallel stops rather than snowplough stops. We went higher up and did some easy red runs. As we were getting hungry, we headed to one of the resort's restaurant buffet, joining Boris, Sean and Tim already seated. Celek greeted Boris like her long-lost lover, smothering him in kisses. Tim and Graham enjoyed being surrounded by three lovely young ladies. We ordered, and all sat in the sun eating.

***

Celek wanted Boris and Tim to join us that afternoon. Tim was more than happy to ski with a bevvy of ladies. We all skied down to drop Graham off at the hotel and bounced back up the mountain on a chairlift. The afternoon was fun with the six of us enjoying our time out.

We had explained Tim's learning difficulties to the girls, and they semi-adopted him. They got him to show them how to ski and laughing at his corny jokes. Tim was having a ball, whilst Boris and I enjoyed the girl's company quite differently, as all three of them wore tight ski gear and each of us getting kisses upon demand.

We made our way to the après-ski bar in the late afternoon to grab a large table and some beers whilst waiting for Petri and the others to arrive. The girls tried to teach Tim some dance moves but his awkward tall frame and lack of coordination making him dance more like my dad. The girls were understanding, continuing to dance and fuss over him.

***

Petri arrived with the others and we all caught up on each other group's day. I got each of us a double round of shots. Tim started getting weary and wanted to go back to the hotel. Katrina's brother, while Tim went to the restroom, invited Boris and I to join him and the group for dinner at a steakhouse in centre of town. They had already made reservations. Petri told us that the steakhouse had an après-ski bar underneath, and he would be grateful if we came.

This choice was simple, Boris and I gulped our shots down and took Tim to the hotel. We changed as fast as we could, explaining to the guys we had to make good on a promise again with Petri. I told Tim I'd be back before morning as Boris and I ran out the door.

* * *

We found the steakhouse with ease. Finding our Polish friends already encamped at a bar table with rows of shots. Katrina and Celek waved as they saw us approaching and made room for us to squeeze in.

The atmosphere was exciting, the music was thumping and the group knew how to dance and sing to any American song they recognised.

While waiting for the seating arrangements upstairs, I ordered us two large pizzas and garlic bread along with some more shots. This turned out to be a bad choice as the bill came to half a fortune. Thankfully, my credit card could cope.

* * *

Drinks were flowing, and the ladies had started some kind of drinking game that they couldn't explain to us in English. Katrina and Celek were either losing or struggling to keep up with the other girls. At the end of the game, both were by far the worse for drink. I got the girls Pepsis, but it didn't make a dent in their conditions.

By the time we had moved up to our section upstairs in the steakhouse, Katrina and Celek were drunk as fuck so we had to half carry them up. Katrina's dad was not amused and had a few words with her brother. Celek started eating some of her starters, but Katrina fell asleep as soon as the food arrived. We tried to keep her awake, but she was beat after several days of skiing and heavy drinking. Katrina did eat a little, but after several bites, she dashed to the ladies room. Meanwhile, Petri's wife Elena went to see if she was okay. When she returned, she escorted me to go the ladies' room door and told me to take her sister-in-law home.

* * *

I found Katrina slumped in a chair near the toilets,

singing something Polish in a drunken stupor. Putting my coat on first, I handed her hers. Then I managed to half carry and lead her outside to the chalet. The long walk helped sober Katrina up a little or so I thought.

We reached her place minutes later and as soon as Katrina took off her jacket, she ran to the toilet to throw up. I followed behind her and quickly moved her ponytail out of the way of the toilet while she did so. She then stood up and started peeing almost in my direction. I pulled her in the right direction and the bottom part of her shirt was wet. I struggled to get her panties down as somehow she lost control of her powerful stream.

Finally, I cleaned Katrina up, got her dressed and into bed. She curled up in the fetal position and dozed off to sleep rather quickly. Covering her with the duvet, I put on a bedside light. Then, I found an old plastic bowl in the kitchen to leave close by her just in case she needed to vomit again.

Nearly an hour later, Katrina's parents, Celek, Boris and Petri returned. They woke me up as they made their way through the house, everyone speaking in typical drunken whispers that would wake the deceased. Katrina was snoring heavily as a shaft of light from the opening door broke into the room. Celek crept inside while Boris was embracing her. I motioned with a hushing gesture to my lips. They giggled and backed out closing the door behind them.

Chapter Eight

My phone's alarm went off at seven and I made my way back to my hotel to find Tim getting dressed. I found Boris in the breakfast area confirming that Celek had kicked him out again as soon as they had done the deed. We had breakfast and went out to the slopes to meet with Graham. Higher winds had picked up, and the sky was cloudier today. As a result, we all skied lower down at a medium height to keep out of the wind. At ten, we dropped by the pop up après-ski bar to find everyone else but Katrina, ready to start skiing.

Celek greeted me with a big hug. She thanked me for choosing to be a gentleman and taking care of her friend last night. Katrina had too big of a hangover to come along with us. Therefore, Sean, Boris, Celek, Marzena, Tim and I caught the lift to ski for the day together.

* * *

At the lunch, whilst Marzena and Celek went to order their food, Boris and I compared notes. On the first day, Celek had also pestered Boris about his phone contact details, but since then, nothing more, even when the opportunity arose. We were both relieved, as they seemed to have given up their interrogations, with our anonymity still intact.

Over lunch, I made the mistake to ask Celek to see if Katrina wanted to meet up this afternoon or if she wanted to hang out for dinner.

"You text her and ask?" She answered, grinning, knowing that I should have already known the answer.

Pulling my phone out, she dictated the number to me, starting with the Polish country code.

Shortly after, Katrina texted me back saying she still felt ill. A second text followed, saying she would like company if I wanted to visit after skiing. Boris kicked me under the table and gave me a weird look. I told him to knock it off.

* * *

We had a good afternoon and visited the same après-ski bar up on the mountain for a few shorts. I skied back to the hotel with Tim, leaving Boris with Celek. I showered and changed, before walking up to the chalet.

Katrina must have seen me walking up as she was waiting for me at the door. She was pale looking and dressed in joggers and a baggy fleece but pleased to see me.

"Haha, you text me now. You could have called."

"I didn't know whether I was disturbing you," I replied as she escorted me through back to the games room to a large sofa. She re-started a TV show she was watching and selected English sub-titles for me, curling up on my lap to watch. It was some kind of detective story, but being halfway through, I couldn't get into it, although she tried to help to explain. It was nice to be alone together to talk and not have to fight for her attention amongst an onslaught of Polish group chatter.

"He is the killer; they are trying to catch him. But he is better than the police." She tried to explain the obvious scene shown on the TV.

"The man with the gun? Ha-ha, I guessed, thanks." I answered sarcastically.

"Is he the good guy?" I continued to probe, pointing at one of the other characters.

"No." Katrina looked at me, pulling a mock annoyed face, slapping me on my leg.

"Is he?" I teased back, half tickling her.

"No, watch and learn. You are useless." She laughed back, smiling.

"Ha ha, sorry," I apologised, giving her a squeeze.

After a while she realised it was useless and remained quiet. When the show ended, I realised she had dozed off again, so I let her sleep, whilst the TV went on to the next episode.

* * *

I must have dozed off myself as her dad's laughter woke me. He then called out to us saying that dinner was ready. When we came down, Katrina's father and mother were the only ones who dined with us. Meanwhile, Petri, Celek, Boris and the others were out at the après-ski bar. Over dinner, our conversation was lively, discussing anything and everything; family legacies, employment, politics and European history were all on the talble. Katrina didn't eat too much or drink, but I had my fill along with a few glasses of champagne.

After dinner, Katrina and I went back to the games room and put on Netflix. Katrina put on a film I didn't recognise, with English subtitles. She then put her legs across my lap and reclined on me.

"Mmm, this looks nice," she said minutes after the movie started.

"Yes, it looks good. How do you feel?"

"Much better, my head and stomach are not aching me anymore. Thank you for looking after me last night. It was very nice. Celek said you had slept on the sofa? Men in our town would not have been so nice, thank you."

"Can you remember being sick? You were like a firehose I had to hold your hair clear." I grinned.

"No, don't tease me. Thanks, but I could taste and smell it in the morning, yuk." She smiled and gave me a slap, then made a finger in her mouth, mimicking making herself sick, then laughed.

"Can you remember peeing on my hand?"

"Noooo, I didn't?"

"Yes, you did, after you were sick. I sat you on the toilet, but you peed without warning, so I had to pull your boxers down."

"I don't wear boxers," She squealed.

"So you put my pyjamas on?" She asked, looking at me questioningly.

"Yes, but I had to dry you first. It was funny, you were all floppy and your boobies kept getting in the way!" I teased, laughing to be sure she realised I was joking.

"Nooo, not my boobs. Ha-ha, you're lying. Thanks for my pyjamas. I thought it may have been Celek who clothed me, thank you, but it was nice to wake up dressed. Did you also put the bowl there?"

"Yes, I didn't want you to vomit on the sheets!" I teased.

"Sheesh, it's embarrassing."

"So, no more drinking games with Celek, Marzena and the others?"

"No," She agreed. "Papa was not happy. Papa, my mom and brother want me to find a husband. My papa said you wouldn't want a wife who drinks too much."

Panic crept back in after such a good start to the evening, I have no desire for a shotgun wedding.

Katrina must have felt me tense up and looked up to see my face, "haha, don't worry. I don't want a husband. I...I just want to be free for a few years, to finish school and travel."

"Phew!" I relaxed.

* * *

We continued chatting whilst half-watching the movie. Katrina was happy to talk about her life and what she wanted to do.

After a few days of skiing and drinking, it felt good to have a quiet night just the two of us, like Ken and Barbie in the dollhouse.

As the clock ticked passed ten, Katrina said, "I want to go to bed. No sex tonight, I'm so tired. Are you staying? I don't want to be alone."

"I can," I answered.

Shortly after, we went to Katrina's bedroom and curled up in bed. Not long after, I felt a nude Celek slide into bed with us on Katrina's side. She kissed me and ran her fingers through my hair, and then soon, we all dozed off to sleep.

Chapter Nine

Katrina awoke me with kisses. She had more colour in her face this morning, chaperoning her lovely smile. Celek's face popped over her shoulder to kiss us. I felt someone's hand stroking my morning wood, without knowing whose it was. It felt like any sleepover, chatting and rubbing each other.

Today was my supposedly final day on the trip. Katrina's brother, Petri told me before that his family were staying until Sunday then they would take the long drive home to Poland. I texted Katrina asking if I could stay with her on my last night and she was delighted. The others on my trip and Boris were to leave for the airport at five in the morning Saturday and I would have to check out the hotel at the same time.

Because I am driving all the way back to the UK, I

wanted a lie-in. Honestly, I didn't have to leave until later in the day. Celek looked disappointed and surprisingly didn't ask about what Boris would do.

For me, it was a late breakfast in the chalet with Katrina and Celek and then to the pop-up bar. Boris, Sean, and Tim were already awaiting me. Last day, so we don't want any last-minute heroics or injuries, so Boris and I discussed routes to the group in detail. We set off with our merry band of seven, my last day to be with my Barbie.

* * *

Cloudier skies gave poor sunlight conditions for Sean, so he decided by mid-day to call it quits and return to the hotel to pack early. We dropped him off at the nearest point to the hotel where a shuttle picked him up and the rest of us returned skiing.

Like previous days, we hit the après-ski bar up on the mountain by the end of the afternoon. Meanwhile, Katrina and Celek weren't as keen to keep up with us, clearly aggrieved by our departures. By the end of our day out, I dropped Tim off, showered, changed into something casual and had most of my bags packed. I checked out of the hotel to load my skis, boots and gear into my works van. Then, I made my way to the bar with Boris to join the group for one last outing.

***

The night went as planned; lots of shots, merriment, singing, dancing, pizzas, and a cab ride back to Katrina's chalet. Celek and Katrina repeated Tuesday's fun in the hot tub, with lots of champagne and music. They teased us to jerk off in the tub in front of them. Stupidly, Boris and I had done so.

Afterwards, we all together for a five-star dinner, enjoying many courses washed down with wine and beer, to finish with lattes and a round of karaoke in the games room. After several songs, I lost track of time, to realise that Boris and Celek had once again disappeared. Katrina pulled me to the side and escorted me to her hotel room.

***

Once inside, Katrina made no pretence, turning the light off as she quickly closed the door. We kissed, starting on each other's lips then working our way around each other as we stripped. She then pushed her lovely round bum right down on my throbbing cock. I kissed her neck as she bounced to the music still playing a few rooms away.

My hands fondled Katrina's lovely small mounds and button nipples which caused her to make expressive moans. From the back, my tongue made its way down; kissing her shoulders, then to her collarbone. Katrina reached back downwards, grabbing my cock, as I pushed her forward onto the bed.

* * *

I spread Katrina's legs, kissing between them until I reached her little maker's nameplate sat on her bridge. I felt her throbbings, as I made my way down her ridge to her purse, finding her wet and resting my nose on what little pubic hair she had. My tongue pierced open up her lips to find Katrina's sweet sappy nectar.

Katrina's hands grasped through my hair as she moaned, "ohhhhh!" Her sounds kept my tongue engaged. She arched her back as my tongue worked its way around her pussy, firing all her cylinders, making her hips rise. Katrina's pussy was flooding inside my mouth as her bud was inviting upwards to suck on it.

I decided to allow my finger to follow the spring trickle to its source as my tongue's created a violent spasm through Katrina. She moaned my name and was grunting heavily. I then sucked and nibbled at her nub as my hands went upwards, grazing her hard nipples which brought out the same result of Katrina's writhing. I was so excited myself that my pre-cum could have mistaken for the real thing just by listening to Katrina's soundtracks of pleasure.

"Mmmmm, do it to me with your two fingers, please, mmm..." Katrina grunted.

I slid both my fingers quickly inside her while my thumb flicked her cunt. Katrina spasmed, stifling a scream, "Oh, oh, oh, fuck, I'm..." She tried pulling my hand away but I held steady until she came down off her orgasm.

***

"That was so good Dave, put on condom. Do me..."

That was the best English Katrina had spoken since I met her.

I scrabbled through my pockets and stood up to slide it on. Meanwhile, Katrina began masturbating. She spasmed almost immediately, squirting in my direction. *Oh my god, she looks so fucking hot!*

Next, I entered Katrina, feeling underneath the sheets her pussy juice. She wrapped her legs around me and I pumped in and out, her wetness slouching as I drove myself between her sexy buttcheeks. My excitement from Katrina's recent orgasm had me already on edge. Her pussy's clutched my cock as her silky body continued squirming but matching my thrusts. Her mouth opened say the following: "Fuck me, woow, mmph, oh, oh, oh, umph, umph, that's it, that's it..."

Katrina's cunt squeezed the dick tighter. Her climax was building making her arch her back once again, "Yeeeeeessss, yes, Dave...Oh, fuck..." Feeling her second wave, I joined in and came with her, kissing her as I did so passionately in the mouth.

We were panting out of breath as Katrina unwrapped her legs around me. I got up, threw the condom in the toilet and returned quickly. We intertwined; kissing and cuddling as we played with each other's fingers. Within minutes, we fell asleep, my mind flashing back to the memories of this trip so far.

***

In the wee hours of the night, I heard the bedroom door click then open and close gently. Feeling the weight of an extra body in the bed, I knew it was Celek who now joined us under the duvet. She kissed me first then laid beside Katrina. I heard her kissing her, Celek moaning while my girl kissed her back. These weren't little pecks on the cheek; these were sloppy fiery smooches.

With that, there was lots of rustling as hands roamed between them, making me realise I was the third wheel on this bicycle. Katrina got on top of Celek and they were making out.

Katrina sucked on Celek's bosoms which were glistening with her saliva. Celek's hands were guiding

Katrina where she wanted them as she looked at me and nodded. I slipped over, kissing and palming her round ass. She was filled with sexual tension as Katrina began eating her out.

The duvet was now flung off, Katrina's bum was in the air, bobbing up and down as she went to work. Her friend was ecstatic, moving her head from side to side.

"Dave, fuck Katy like doggie?" Celek requested, her eyes bulging out their sockets.

I nodded okay and jumped up to get my last condom.

My cock was already hard and straight for me to slip it on. Katrina widen her stance to welcome me in as I came up from behind her. She was wet as heck when my cock slipped in her. We bumped and ground for a few strokes while Celek and I had made eye contact.

"Fuck, fuck..." Celek panted as Katrina kept licking away. Katrina, in the meantime, backed into me as fast as she can.

"Oh, Dave...right...there..." she moaned as we worked with each other in unison. I saw Celek's boobs bouncing up and down. her mouth went between ecstatic 'O' to a broad grin, her eyes looked like dinner plates. She kept saying fuck and I grinned knowing that my Barbie gave her friend the best lick job she could desire.

Minutes later

I don't know who came first, but Katrina got off me and they started eating each other out. Together, they groaned yelling each other names which seemed to be at the same time. I came eventually on their tits and the girls were quick to clean me off. Then once again, we were all drifting off to sleep.

Chapter Ten

The noise of the chalet awakening and the morning sun trying to break through the curtains woke the three of us. We cuddled and kissed each other in the morning's sun kiss.

Katrina whispered in Polish to Celek, which caused her to burst into a squeal of joy, hugging and kissing her passionately.

This turned out to be an awesome vacation!

Celek told me that she and Katrina were childhood friends, but over the last year ago, they had become secret lovers. Celek wanted them to both come out of the closet, to confess their love for each other in front of their families. She wanted them to both commit to each other and to move to London, being more cosmopolitan than the small Polish town they currently live in, where they could live freely without prejudice.

But Katrina was afraid. Whilst Celek could make that decision, having previously lost her virginity at an early age and travelled the world, she could commit with confidence. But Katrina didn't have the luxury to do so yet. Her father's influence in Poland and her brother deterred even the most determined admirer whether it be male or female.

So not only shying away from the anguish it would bring to her family, even possible exile from it, Katrina felt she couldn't commit to such a life-changing decision as of yet.

Terrified that later Katrina may inflict pain on Celek if she left her to move on without her. Unlike selecting the wrong paint colour, such a commitment, would leave them both unable to press any imaginary 'reset' button.

* * *

When I saved Katrina on the piste, she plotted her scheme to make her family approve of me because it would look like a traditionally heterosexual romance. Katrina chose to seduce me, to help her spend intimate time with Celek.

Celek was keen to apologise, saying it was actually my tongue that confirmed to Katrina that she didn't need a phallus inside her to rock her world. She also used Boris as a ploy to make it seemed like she was heterosexual. When

Boris couldn't give her satisfaction, she sought me. The girls realised the irony of the situation, saying they both loved me and thanked me dearly. They couldn't have wished for a more fit gentleman to be a guinea pig for their secret holiday getaway.

They insisted that we keep in touch and hopefully, we'll meet up in London or somewhere else in the world one day.

I had a lot to ponder on during my long drive home. Despite having experienced this wild ride for the week, I was still unsure about how I felt about the situation. I was sure though that I would choose not to tell Boris how the story really ended.

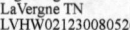
www.ingramcontent.com/pod-product-compliance
Lightning Source LLC
LaVergne TN
LVHW021230080526
838199LV00089B/5982